Emily Arnold McCully

THE
BOBBIN GIRL

New York Dial Books for Young Readers

Published by Dial Books for Young Readers
A member of Penguin Putnam Inc.
375 Hudson Street
New York, New York 10014

Special thanks to the staff of the Museum of American
Textile History for their help in checking the facts in this book;
and to Gail Mohanty, curator of Slater Mill Historic Site,
for sharing her expertise on bobbins and spinning frames.
Typography by Atha Tehon
Printed in Hong Kong
First Edition
10

Library of Congress Cataloging in Publication Data
McCully, Emily Arnold.
The bobbin girl / Emily Arnold McCully.—1st ed.
p.   cm.
Summary: A ten-year-old bobbin girl working in a textile mill in
Lowell, Massachusetts, in the 1830's, must make a difficult decision—
will she participate in the first workers' strike in Lowell?
ISBN 0-8037-1827-6.—ISBN 0-8037-1828-4 (lib.)
[1. Textile workers—Fiction. 2. Strikes and lockouts—Textile workers—Fiction.
3. Children—Employment—Fiction. 4. Lowell (Mass.)—Fiction.] I. Title.
PZ7.M478415Bo   1996   [Fic]—dc20   95-6997   CIP   AC

The artwork was rendered in watercolor on watercolor paper with pastel highlights.

— For Doreen —

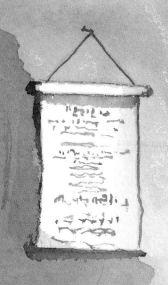

On Saturday, when the line of mill girls passed through the paymaster's office, the youngest was too small to reach the ledger to sign her name: *Rebecca Putney, Bobbin Girl.* Ten-year-old Rebecca took her wages and raced home to give them to her mother. Mrs. Putney, a widow, ran a company boardinghouse. Generous with her meals and comforts, she struggled to pay her bills.

"With your help we'll be able to make ends meet," she said. Rebecca beamed proudly. It was exciting to be in Lowell, the City of Spindles, with a job to do.

The mill girls' days were ruled by bells. The first rang from the mill's great bell tower on Monday at 4:30 A.M. Rebecca struggled awake. Everyone had to be at their machines by the next bell, at 5:30. The rules were strict. Girls who were late or who made mistakes were dismissed. Rebecca was never late. Her mother and the girls in the spinning room depended on her.

At 5:30 the machines all started at once with an earsplitting racket. The great building shuddered. The spindles and looms in row after row were

relentless monsters with lives of their own! Beside them the young women looked frail and powerless to Rebecca. But it was up to them to make everything run smoothly.

Rebecca's task took just fifteen minutes every hour. She worked in Spinning Room #2, removing full bobbins of yarn from the spinning frames and replacing them with empty ones.

She was supposed to sit quietly in the corner of the hot, damp room until the bobbins filled up. But at mid-morning she checked to see if Mr. Capshaw, the overseer, was at his desk. When he wasn't looking, she slipped outside. Her ears rang—they rang in her dreams!—but it was quieter in the yard.

Hidden in the wall was the book her friend Judith had given her, *Gulliver's Travels.* Judith had said it was important to stretch her mind. The mill girls were all improving their minds. It was called Lowell Fever. The corporation forbade reading inside the mill, but the girls taped printed sheets and even math to their looms and the windows to study while they worked.

When the dinner bell rang at noon, the machines stopped and everyone dashed to their boardinghouses. Rebecca had only half an hour to get home, wolf down the huge meal her mother had cooked for her boarders, and return to the mill. Her little sisters and brother helped to serve.

Next to Rebecca sat Kezia, who had come to earn money for a dowry. Ruth had run away from a father who beat her. Huldah was paying off the mortgage on her family's farm. Another girl saved money for her brother's tuition at Harvard.

Judith, who sat across the table, was Rebecca's idol. She was a weaver and earned $1.75 a week, half of which she deposited in the savings bank. "There is an academy that will take women students," she had told Rebecca. "I intend to enroll as soon as I have saved the tuition." Judith was so sure of herself, Rebecca marveled. Even on this brief break for dinner she sat with an open book.

When she had free time that afternoon, Rebecca went up to Judith's weaving room. It was almost as hot as the spinning room. Lint clouded the moist air, kept humid so the cotton thread wouldn't break. Judith tended two looms here; Ruth stood nearby. She glanced at Rebecca, who waved.

Then Ruth began to cough. She coughed so hard, she doubled over, gasping for breath.

There was a bucket of water in the doorway. Rebecca wanted to carry a cup to Ruth—but if Mr. Capshaw caught her away from her bobbins, he would be furious. The girls around Ruth looked worried, but they dared not leave their looms.

Suddenly Judith was at Ruth's side, supporting her. Mr. Capshaw burst in. He gestured angrily for Ruth to sit and for Judith to take over her looms. Behind him Judith's mouth widened in an angry torrent of words that could not be heard above the din. Rebecca slipped out of the room unnoticed.

The day finally ended after thirteen and a half hours, at 7:00 P.M.
At home Ruth had another fit of coughing. Several heads turned in alarm.
A new lung disease had attacked many in the mills. Everyone believed that
it was caused by breathing the wet, lint-filled air. Ruth blushed at the
attention. "It's just a little cold!" she said. Rebecca saw that she was afraid
of being sick and felt ashamed for not daring to comfort her earlier.

"But you must see the doctor," Judith said. "It's a crime they make us
work with the windows nailed shut! We are all at risk, not only yourself."

"Hush, Judith," Huldah said. "Would you rather be a housemaid somewhere? Where else can a woman earn a real wage? And would you give up your Lyceum lectures and your Literary Society and your German class?"

"You know I would not," Judith said. "But I needn't accept indifference and illness along with them."

After supper the mood was cheerful. Now at last they were free until 10:00. One group went off to hear a lecture, another went to the shops. A few wrote letters or sewed in the parlor. Rebecca studied a geography textbook, just as if she were going to school.

As the ten o'clock curfew approached, girls began straggling back. Finally everyone was present, chattering about the evening's events—everyone except Judith.

"She is so headstrong!" Mrs. Putney worried. She opened the door and leaned out, scanning the street for a sign of the wayward Judith.

"There she is!" cried Rebecca, peering too. Judith ran up the steps.

"I'm sorry, Mother Putney," she said. "I was speaking with Mr. Emerson after the lecture. Oh, he is inspiring! His topic was Self-Reliance. He says that most people think being good means following the crowd. But true goodness lies in the courage of self-reliance. I feel so fortunate to have heard him!"

Self-reliance! The words rang in Rebecca's head. They described Judith herself. She spoke her mind and did what she thought right, no matter what the consequences! Rebecca vowed to be self-reliant too.

The next day as Rebecca passed the weaving room, there was a commotion. Mr. Capshaw ran out and pushed her aside, muttering, "Get away, child!" Two more men bounded up, rushed into the room, and emerged carrying something—a person! All the while the machines clanked on.

Rebecca waited anxiously for Judith when the dinner bell rang. "A shuttle flew off the loom and hit Ruth. She had turned away to cough," the older girl told her.

"Oh, no! Is she badly hurt?"

Judith was very angry. "It grazed her head and knocked her out. This isn't the first time, you know. When there are accidents, they never tell us. They don't even stop the machines."

At the end of the day Mrs. Putney said, "Ruth is at the doctor's. Take her some soup, Rebecca. She'll need her strength."

So Rebecca took the soup and walked six blocks to the doctor's house.

"She won't be able to eat that yet," said the doctor's wife gruffly. "But you may bid her good evening."

Ruth was very pale. She looked at Rebecca and tears poured from her eyes.

"Oh, Ruth, I'm so sorry," Rebecca said.

"You don't even know..." Ruth answered, and began to sob. Finally she blurted out the whole story.

When Rebecca returned to the boardinghouse, the girls were waiting in the parlor. "Ruth has been sent home," she told them. "Mr. Capshaw says she may not return to this or any other mill. She is called 'careless.'"

"But the accident was not her fault!" Judith cried.

"She has nowhere to go but to the father who beats her," said Mrs. Putney softly. All faces turned to her, aghast.

There was a loud knock on the door. Rebecca opened it to admit a friend of Judith's from the Merrimack Mill. She was very agitated.

"The owners have met in Boston. They claim the price of cotton cloth has fallen. They are to lower our wages—by fifteen percent, some say!" Everyone gasped. Some were disbelieving.

But Judith was convinced it was true. "We can stop them!" she declared hotly. "We must stand together. We will not be factory slaves, never to earn enough for a better life!"

No! We will not! thought Rebecca. But then she saw her mother's worried face. Girls who made trouble for the mill owners lost their jobs.

Judith went on, her voice ringing, "Let us hold a meeting tomorrow at the dinner break!"

"Hear, hear!" Kezia shouted.

Mrs. Putney said, "I am so afraid they will dismiss anyone who attends a meeting."

"It seems to me we must take the chance," Judith declared. "Come to Spinning Room Number One, all who agree."

The official notice of reduced wages was posted the next morning. When the dinner bell rang, hundreds of mill girls crowded into Spinning Room #1. A sign hung outside: No Men Allowed. Judith called the meeting to order.

"Here is a petition," Judith announced. "It pledges that we will never work for reduced wages! Sign it, and I will take it to the overseer." The petition was passed from girl to girl.

Huldah cried out, "Don't sign! The mill owners will not forgive traitors. I cannot afford to lose my job. Which of you can?"

There was a great clamor of voices. "I cannot! My family will starve!" someone called out. "But we must not let them crush us!" someone else cried. "What should we do?" "Sign!" "Don't sign!"

Mr. Capshaw tried to force his way in. "Order!" he bellowed. "Let us respect order or our society will collapse!"

Voices cried, "OUT! OUT!" and he backed away.

Judith said, "Take heart! The owners choose to reduce our wages because they think we are powerless. But if we stand together, we will win! Justice is on our side!" Rebecca gazed at her with pride. Had any woman ever spoken so stirringly? Many faces were alight with determination, but some were still fearful. Huldah wept. Not everyone was willing to sign the petition. The bell rang then and all rushed back to their machines.

In Spinning Room #2 they waited breathlessly to see what would happen after Judith gave the petition to Mr. Capshaw. Suddenly a girl at a window cried out. Judith was down in the yard! Everyone ran to see. Judith waved her bonnet wildly to all the windows of the mill.

"She's been dismissed!" Kezia cried. They all stared at Judith, shocked into silence. And then, across the courtyard a door opened. First one, then two, six, dozens of girls streamed across the yard to stand with Judith. Rebecca watched, unable to separate her fear for them from her excitement.

"They're turning out! They're standing by her!" someone said.

Kezia turned off her loom. Down the row, Lucy shut hers off. A moment later every machine in the mill was silenced. It seemed to Rebecca almost as if the world were coming to an end.

At first no one spoke. Then Lucy said, "She is waving at us to come. What should we do?"

"Will you go down?" "I'm afraid."

There was a buzz of voices, but no one moved.

Rebecca saw Mr. Capshaw at the door. Suddenly she remembered Judith coming home from Mr. Emerson's lecture. *The courage of self-reliance!* She heard herself shout, "*I* am going to turn out, whether anyone else does or not!" Her words echoed in the vast room.

She marched out of the room, past Mr. Capshaw, and down the stairs. She looked behind her. A line of girls from Spinning Room #2 followed her all the way to the yard. She had led them *all* out!

The mill girls paraded through the town to Chapel Hill, where Judith gave a fiery speech. "Our grandfathers fought for independence in the Revolution! We stand in the spirit of their sacrifice! Never will the daughters of free men be factory slaves! Give us the wages we are due or we will not work at all!"

Never before in Lowell had a woman spoken in public to a crowd. Rebecca was stunned.

Judith next called upon the mill girls to march to the bank and withdraw their savings. The bank was soon emptied of its funds. Each girl pledged five dollars so those without savings could go home to their farms.

At suppertime some girls were already packing. Kezia said, "Ruth can come with me. She won't have to face her brutal father." Everyone wondered how long the turnout would last. Would the owners give in and restore the workers' full pay?

Huldah had sat apart. Now she said, "I am going back to the mill tomorrow. I have no choice." The room was quiet. Rebecca looked at her mother anxiously.

"Do what is right, my dear," her mother said. "We will find a way to live."

So Rebecca stayed home all the rest of the week. Each day more girls returned to the mill or left Lowell to go back to their farms. The mill owners did not give in.

On Sunday Mrs. Putney was told to expect the arrival of some girls from New Hampshire, replacements for those who had gone home. Judith was silent and preoccupied at the news. When she went up to her room after supper, Rebecca followed and found her packing her bag.

"What are you doing?" Rebecca cried.

"The turnout failed," Judith said. "There are too many girls like Huldah who feel they must work. I'm going to find a position in another town."

Rebecca gasped. It was as if she'd been hit by a flying shuttle. Judith had led her into battle, and now she was deserting!

Judith saw her expression and said gently, "We are not defeated, Rebecca. We showed we can stand up for what is right. Next time, or the time after, we will win."

"But for now…" Rebecca began.

"For now you must go back to work. You must save your money. I will be working to improve our conditions somewhere else. Can you take my place here in Lowell?"

Judith's confidence in her made Rebecca's heart swell to bursting. "I will do everything I can," she promised. "Everything you would do!"

Judith shut her bag and picked up her bonnet. Rebecca smiled as her friend suddenly shook the bonnet at the silent bell tower in a last defiant wave. Then, with a hug for Rebecca, she was gone.

Author's Note

Lowell, Massachusetts, was established in 1826. The first planned industrial city, it was founded entirely for the purpose of manufacturing cloth. Here, every operation—from opening the bale of cotton, picking out the foreign matter, carding the fibers, and spinning the yarn to weaving and finishing the fabric—could be performed by machines under one roof. Girls from farms and villages all around New England flocked to Lowell to work in the new industry. The mill owners hired women rather than men because they would work for lower wages. Even so, women earned more in the mills than they could anywhere else. They lived and worked together in a powerful common experience, eagerly improving their minds at a time when no college would grant a woman a degree.

The bobbin girl Rebecca Putney was loosely inspired by Harriet Hanson Robinson (1825–1911), whose widowed mother came from Boston to Lowell to run a mill boardinghouse. At the age of ten, in 1835, Harriet began work as a bobbin girl, or "doffer." (The term comes from the phrase "doing off," or removing filled bobbins.)

In 1834 the mill owners had lowered the women's wages, confident they would accept the reduction. Instead many "turned out." They were replaced by new recruits from the country-side, and mill operation returned to normal. But the precedent had been set: Workers could rebel if they were unfairly treated. My story treats this first workers' strike in Lowell, but Harriet Hanson Robinson actually took part in the next one, in 1836. That year, management announced that workers would be charged a new fee for board, reducing their take-home pay again. Young Harriet herself led the turnout from her spinning room at the Lawrence Mill. She later described it as the proudest moment of her life.

In the decades following Harriet's action, the mill owners took ruthless steps to increase pro-duction and profits. Workers tended more machines for lower pay. Machines were speeded up. Overseers whose workers produced the most were awarded bonuses. Clocks were secretly slowed to extend the workday. More turnouts resulted, and a ten-hour-day movement swept factories. Workers demanded to be treated as people, not machines, in a fight led by women.

Harriet Hanson Robinson remained a mill girl for many years. She married a newspaper editor and was active in the battles to abolish slavery and give women the vote. She re-counted her early experiences in her 1898 memoir, *Loom and Spindle; or, Life Among the Early Mill Girls.*